Norman La Marsh

Lux Christi

A Sacred Drama

Norman La Marsh

Lux Christi
A Sacred Drama

ISBN/EAN: 9783337376673

Printed in Europe, USA, Canada, Australia, Japan

Cover: Foto ©Andreas Hilbeck / pixelio.de

More available books at **www.hansebooks.com**

𝕷𝖚𝖝 𝕮𝖍𝖗𝖎𝖘𝖙𝖎

A SACRED DRAMA

BY

NORMAN LAMARSH

I am the light of the world: he that followeth me shall not walk in darkness, but shall have the light of life.—Jesus.

SECOND EDITION

BANGOR
DAILY NEWS JOB PRINTING OFFICE
1895

AFFECTIONATELY

DEDICATED

TO

Alice Lane LaMarsh,

BY THE AUTHOR.

PROEM.

In launching this tiny volume on the sea of public opinion, we are fully conscious that it may become waterlogged long before reaching port. It is bound for Heartsboro'; and if it only reach there without the loss of sails, or rudder, or cargo, we shall hope to hear from it again, but if not the loss will be ours.

The task of preparation has been a pleasurable one, because of the restful change it afforded from arduous labor along other lines.

The reader will appreciate the difficulty of the work in hand, when we say that argumentative poetry is not conducive to inspiration; and if there be anything the Muses hate, it is argument.

N. LaMarsh.

Bangor, Me., Jan. 1, 1895.

LUX CHRISTI.

SECTION I.

WASHINGTON, D. C., 9 P. M.

Americus, a gentleman of leisure occupying a suite of rooms at the Arlington, is alone in his private parlor. Having traveled extensively and studied much, he has arrived at the pivotal point of life, which settles or unsettles a man forever, so far as religious belief is concerned. The books on the shelves and center-table are a fitting index of his mental status. Science, philosophy, multitudinous histories, theology, and the authors of standard fiction are all represented. He is seated in a sleepy hollow chair with the light of the Astral lamp falling full on the page before him. Mr. Spencer's latest volume of "Synthetic Philosophy" is the book in question; and the chapter on "The Rights of Free Belief and Worship" is the one now being considered. Like Horace Bushnell, the religious thoughts and intuitions of his boyhood were inspired by a Christian mother; but college life served to dissipate and render void the faith which hitherto had been undisturbed by doubt or subterfuge. His mind is filled with unrest; and he fain would believe that there is something better, nobler, higher than sheer uncertainty.

SOLILOQUY.

Ah, me! no sun, no moon—eternal night!
How drear, how bleak, how dark without the
    light,
Nor would the stars alone suffice to give
The warmth which nature needs to bid it live.
Nay more, the thing called life would droop and
    die
Were sun and moon expunged from nature's sky.
Merely to be extant, do you affirm?
The worms are this,—but who would be a worm?

'Twere better far to never live at all,
Than mid the shades of Erebus to crawl,
Till dissolution come, and then—a blank.
Darkness may be for worms, but not for me,
Since such a thought would seal my destiny.
I crave for light—THE LIGHT, the Light of life,—
Not doubt, not subterfuge, not mental strife.
Moraines may cling to bergs with deathly grip,
Lest from their icy fastenings they slip;
But I, imbued with attributes divine,
Would hate to cling, or crawl, or falsely shine.
This book I hold denies that innate thought
Can be controlled by will, or sold, or bought;
In short, it tells me that belief is based
On principles that cannot be effaced.
Is will not stronger than belief? I ask,
And must I now assume a hopeless task
In striving to return to Christian faith?
And can it be that I am Freedom's slave,
Held by myself, and yet not knowing why?
Or am I only like an aimless wave,
Whose gentle rhythm is nature's lullaby?
O, God, now save me from myself, I pray,
Lest I but fawn and dream and sink away,
Beneath the spell of doubt's etheric draught!
The priceless Book my mother used to read
Was good enough for her,—why not for me!
The faith she cherished answered every need
For life, for death, and for eternity.

SECTION II.

Two members of the diplomatic corps, close friends of Americus, enter. An Oxford Bible is observed among other books on the mahogany center-table. Thesius and Menes have been invited for a purpose: not for the sake of cold argument as might be supposed, but that Americus may strengthen his faith in Christianity by assuming the role of a believer. All three are men of culture, hence no coarseness of argument,—no boisterousness of demeanor, is noticeable in the controversy. Americus contends for the divinity of Christ. The Greek modestly vindicates his faith in the gods. The Egyptian fails to appreciate the mission of One who knew not how to fight. Americus, seated at the table with open Bible, expatiates on the facts contained in the second chapter of St. Matthew's Gospel.

Herod the Great ruled with an iron hand:
His prowess was supreme in all the land,
　As Zion's temple amply testified.
Was it not he who reared those massive walls,
With cloistered precincts and resplendent halls,
Whose dome and minarets evoked such praise?
Aye! he was to blame when the wise men came
In search of the truth respecting a youth,
Whose birth was foretold by prophets of old
Who saw from afar the Bethlehem star,
Appointed of God to lead weary feet,
Over deserts of sand, through rivers fleet,
Over mountains high, under scorching sky,
And　through　gruesome　night,　till　at　last
　　　the Light

For which they searched was found,—the
    Light of life!
And what a wondrous change that Light has
    wrought
O'er art and music, and I know not what;
So that Apollo's brightest light is dim,
When figured closely side by side with Him.
The same is true of Amun's ancient lore,
Whose fetish light must fade to shine no more.
And when we pass from gods to mortal men,
Though they possess a Cyclopean brain,
Their ethics are but cold and meaningless,
If they the Light of life do not possess.
The diatribes of Plato, too, are stale,
When heart is heavy, and the visage pale;
And aught that Anaxagoras has said
Is only like a stone, instead of bread.
Not so, however, with the Light of life,
Whose words and spirit counteract all strife,
Bestowing without stint the balm we need,
When otherwise the heart would surely bleed
For lack of balm, not found apart from God.
    (Addressing Thesius.)
I know the gods bespeak oblivion,
As nature's surest balm for mental ills;
But think you would this be elysian
To one whose soul with aspiration fills?
Can something tend toward nothing, is my
    quest,

Or must the spirit die because 'tis hulled?
Think you would such a concept give me rest,
Since death would simply mean to be annulled?
The gods would have me court the Shades, 'tis
      true,
But is it right to die by one's own hand?
No, sir! I swear by yonder heaven so blue,
That such a course would prove the man un-
      manned!
Nor all the arguments of Spartan lore
Could urge me on to seek Nirvana's shore;
That would be worse than death by any foe,
Were he the very lowest of the low.
But to my theme.
Herod was great, but ruled with irksome rod;
And when they told him that a child was born,
Who might be king, it was to him a thorn—
A thorn of keenest sting, which raised his ire:
And there and then, with heart and brain afire,
He vowed to have no rival, were it God.
Had he but known that six brief miles away
The object of his kindled malice lay,
Herod would not have waited till the morn
To rid him well of such a troublous thorn.
      (Menes smiles and says.)
My prophet's riper years bespoke his call
More perfectly than could a burro's stall!
If he, the Nazarene, be Prince of Peace,
Then I my cherished Koran must release.

Sire, your *credo infantum* is absurd!
Avaunt with such a doctrine! On my word
'Twere better to believe a jest than that!
    (Americus continues.)
Why then did Herod seek to kill the babe,
If he were only commonplace? I ask.
Why did he slash promiscuous with blade
Full drawn, and made the keener by his wrath,
If 'twere a common babe he sought to kill?
No, Moslem, no. It was the Son of God
He sought to vanquish and eradicate,
As one who hated with an awful hate.
The child that nestled on its mother's breast
Was not presaged to luxury and rest;
But fiendish plans, though deftly made, were
    spoiled
By One whose purposes are never foiled,
In aught that man can think, or say, or do.
    (Turning to Thesius.)
You say there is no overruling cause,
Apart from those inevitable laws
Which hedge us in like birds forever caged.
Or, like Prometheus, we fain would rise
But cannot, since the prescient fates apprise
Us of our every move with awful gall.
Hark to the voice of Epicurus old,
Whose counsel savors of resistance bold:
Quoth he,—Let appetite and passion reign;
Seek pleasure at all cost—beware of pain;

Indulge thy sportive nature without stint,
Like coins that roll and tumble from the mint;
When others weep, stay thou thyself away,
Their grief will pass, like clouds of yesterday;
Be merry now with Bacchanalian glee;
Resist all forces that would hinder thee;
There is no God behind those changeless fates,
That trig the *summum bonum* of our lives;
Cause and effect are *nil* to him who waits
To steal the hard earned honey from the hives.
No, dear Thesius, no. There was a Hand
That overruled the foibles of a king;
Though swords responded quick to his com-
      mand,
Yet he himself was made to feel the sting.

Against the wary, unrelenting Turk :
And here it was that Ahab made display,
While flagrant Jezebel, his queen, held sway.
Now cast your eyes' to eastward, if you will—
There stands Gilboa, keeping sentry still :
This brings to mind the day when Saul's proud
    steel
Was crushed beneath the crude Philistine's heel.
To north of us is Hermon's lofty peak,
So like a spectre clad in white array ;
And had it but a tongue, methinks 'twould speak
Of what it saw and heard in Jesus' day.
But we must haste, the sable robes of night
Are fast enveloping the transient light ;
And as we now descend to our abode,
It seems to us indeed a sacred road.
Our host, in flowing gaberdine, with grace
Responds to questions asked him of the place,
As to its customs, and traditions old.
He tells us of the shop where Joseph worked,
Around whose memories tradition lurked ;
And when we speak about the Nazarene,
The merits of whose teachings are now seen
Without the aid of mental microscope,
He says—'Tis true that Jesus did live here ;
But as to Messianic gifts—'tis queer
That people will avow belief in him
Whose name to me is but the synonym
For imposition of the direst sort.

SECTION III.

Americus visits Palestine, and tarries several months in personal investigation. Unlike other tourists he spends more time in the quaint old town of Nazareth, than elsewhere. His actual conversion to Christianity is traceable to a dream. The face of Christ makes an indelible impression. He visits Jerusalem, drinks at Jacob's well, bathes his feet in the waters of Gennesaret, clambers to the summit of little Hermon; but none of these have half the charm of Nazareth and its environs. Americus longs for the companionship of his two friends,— the Greek and Moslem, that they may share his new-found joy,—a joy peculiar to Christian belief,—a joy bordering on ecstasy.

We are in Nazareth, a quaint old town,
Mid bleak and barren hills of whitish brown;
Its streets are narrow, running to and fro
With houses of adobe, flat and low;
The town is cleaner than its neighbors old,
And from this lofty point our eyes behold
A varied scene, not soon to be forgot.
To south of us the plains of Jezreel lie,
Peaceful beneath their Oriental sky,
As though they had not heard the din of war:
'Twas on these very plains that Richard strove
To foil the Saracens, who fought like Jove,
That they the holy sepulchre might keep:
'Twas here that Kleber did such valiant work

Whose sky is not surpassed the world around;
And as the zephyrs fanned my heated face,
It seemed as though the angel of God's grace
Kept vigil with the love a mother shows,
Lest harpies might intrude on my repose.
But I must tell you of my dream that night,
That you may share with me the rare delight
Which a congenial dream is wont to make.
I entered Joseph's shop, and there stood Christ,
A lad of seventeen with raven hair
Falling in graceful folds about His neck,
As at the bench he worked with ardent air.
His form was lithe and nimble and each stroke
Of mallet, or of plane, might well provoke
The admiration of a trainéd eye.
O, how I watched him as he moved about,
Afraid to speak, lest I might be in doubt
That it was He whose name I knew so well.
With heart aglow I scarce could wait to ask,
If it were He to whom God gave the task
Of teaching all mankind the way to truth.
He paused.   I then advanced to where He stood,
And as He cast His eyes of liquid brown
Full into mine, I never shall forget
The keenness and the mellowness divine,
Whose lustre was peculiarly their own.
O, blessed thought! I knew at once 'twas He,
The second Person of the Trinity.
He spoke, and said in accents sweet and low—

We listened on, but to no purpose true,
Since what he said came only from a Jew
Whose prejudice was so intense, that faith
And love were qualities he knew not of—
Unless allied to priest and synagogue.
Poor Jew! could he but look beyond himself,—
Beyond his genealogy and pelf,
The scales, perchance, would fall from off his
     eyes,
And he with truer vision realize
That prejudice is costly sacrifice.
What mean the sterile fields of Palestine?
And why such desolation right and left?
Has Phœbus but agreed to dimly shine,
And is the soil of nourishment bereft?
Where now the sciolistic tribes who thought
That God revealed Himself to them alone?
Methinks their destiny was surely fraught
With maledictions of the deepest tone.
God's truth is not expressly for the Jew,
More so than does the soft and glist'ning dew
Refresh the earth in narrow strips or plots:
Nor does the Holy Spirit condescend
To deal with partial grace, and only bend
To those who look on Abram as their friend.

That night, while on the roof of Hadad's house.
I slept the sweetest of all sleeps profound,
Beneath the azure of the Orient,

My mission is not at this bench, you see,
But I must bide the summons ere I go
To tell the world of truest liberty.
'Tis no small task to take the helm of truth—
A task, methinks, forbidden to a youth—
But God will one day give me strength and skill
To steer that craft according to His will.
You think it strange that I should loiter here,
As though my restless soul were insincere;
But truth proclaimed will all the richer be,
When heart and brain have reached maturity.

Pearls do not deck the crest of any wave,
But lie deep down in ocean depths serene,
Far from the leering gloat of shrewdest knave,
Until exhumed by worthy hands, I ween.

When I awoke, the sun had risen high
Above the distant hills which seemed so nigh.
Though eighteen centuries have ta'en their flight,
Since He of whom I dreamed resided here,
The vision of His lovely face last night,
Has given to my soul an uplift clear.
Now as I slake my thirst at Mary's well,
Or clamber to the summit of yon cliff,
My feelings with such rare emotion swell,
That language is a vehicle too stiff
To give expression to exultant thought.
Can words depict the sanctity of love,

Or measure our emotions at their height?
As well might yonder unassuming dove
Bethink itself to chase the eagle's flight.
Oh, the sacredness of our emotion,
When roused from apathy by thoughts divine!
Oh, the blissfulness of our devotion,
When heavenly rays within the sanctum shine!

I left my home in distant Amerique
That I, myself, diviner light might seek;
And O,—I would that Thesius were here,
That he might witness for himself, in clear
And unmistaken light, the truth I feel
Concerning Him who lived for human weal!
And Menes, too, if he could only know
The joy, the peace, the calm that overflow
As in full view of Nazareth I stand,
All doubt would quickly vanish from his mind;
And he, with Thesius, would surely find
The restfulness of soul which I have found,
In quick response to faith that is not bound
By mystic shackles such as bind *them* round.

SECTION IV.

WASHINGTON, 8 P. M.

Americus is again in his own quarters. His suite of rooms at the Arlington is enhanced by the addition of many relics from the Old World. A stone from Jacob's well, a large antique vase from Acre, a finely executed painting of Nazareth, a genuine Damascene sword, and a miniature of the church of the Holy Sepulcher, are among the curios. Thesius and Menes call to extend congratulations, and evince a degree of pleasure, as one relic after another is closely examined and criticised according to merit; but they fail to catch the enthusiasm of their host, whose expressive visage is aglow with interest as he expatiates on the age of this, and the beauty of that. The Greek's observant eye detects a magnificent specimen of the oleander in full bloom, half hidden by the drapery of the French window; and this impresses him more than all else, as Americus readily perceives. The Egyptian, however, is wholly enamoured of the large, ornate vase, which appeals to his knowledge of ancient pottery; and this Americus is not slow to cognize.

The mantel clock now strikes the hour of eight,
As at the door the Greek and Moslem wait
To be admitted by their old-time friend,
Whose long extended sojourn in a land
Nigh to their own, makes them thrice anxious
    now.
            (Americus speaks.)
Ho, Thesius, my friend! and Menes, too!
It gives me unfeigned joy to welcome you,
After so long an absence from my home.

3

(Menes responds.)
Nor is your joy intenser than our own,
For we have missed you, dear Americus.
(Thesius speaks.)
Now tell us all you saw and heard abroad—
The hills you climbed—the valleys that you trod:
Tell us of France and [1]Panama affairs—
What thought you of Parisian life and airs?
Is the Republic safe as now it stands?
Or is it doomed to pass beyond the hands
Of those who pride themselves in vigils strong?
(Americus replies.)
Paris was full of life and gaiety;
A Butterfly each Frenchman seemed to me,
Clutching at pleasure with avidity,
Lest it might slip his hand, as like a boy
Whose airy bubbles give but fleeting joy;
Nor can I speak for French virility,
Which to my mind is instability,
When calmest, coolest judgment is at stake.
While in the chamber of the nation's brains,
With closest scrutiny, I took the pains
To note their methods of procedure bold;
For noise and for excitement based on strife,
I never witnessed ought in all my life
That seemed so much like Satan's carnival;
Men fumed and stamped and raged with cease-
    less yell,
Condemning everything 'twixt heaven and hell

1 1892 Panama canal scandal at its height.

That had to do with Panama affairs.
The truth is this,—men often lose their head,
When coolness would the better serve instead.
(Thesius speaks.)
Now pardon me, sire, the same fault is here;
On the floor of the House men often cheer,
And resort to other ungainly freaks
To defeat the purpose of him who speaks;
And does this not indicate lack of brains,
Since those who distract will not take the pains
To analyze thought apart from their own?
(Americus replies.)
Not always, my friend, although I confess,
That vulgar applause should meet with repress.
(Menes speaks.)
Well said, Americus, your words are true;
By Cheops pyramid! I like that view;
And though I worship Allah, still I feel
That men of Christ should always be genteel.
(Thesius turns the conversation.)
Whence did you lovely oleander come?
Was it the landlord's gift to grace your room?
Its flowers, methinks, I never saw surpassed;
And could I be assured that they would last,
The gift would all the more intrinsic be;
But they must lose their bloom, and so must we.
Oh, how I hate the thought that I must die!
And were it in my province to reply,
I fain would stamp so direful a decree

With maledictions full of irony.
You cannot make me think your God is good,
Unless his mandates can be understood
To mean precisely what you say they do.
Instance this lovely flower: why must it fade,
As though its very life were only made
To turn our love of beauty into scorn?
And as for Christian faith, I cannot see
What value such a faith would be to me,
Since it ignores my right to think and act,
As though the future were a settled fact.
Oh! for some quiet spot in Tempe's vale,
Where loveliness personified exists!
Then I would gladly banish every trail
Of that which now my soul so keen resists:
O, death! where is thy sting? It has a sting
Which even Christ himself could not evade;
O, grave! where is thy victory, you sing,
As though our soul-life were not doomed to fade.
                    (Menes speaks.)
Well said, dear Thesius, agreed with you;
A faith that changes yellow into blue,
Or *red* to *white*, is to abstruse for me,
No matter what the consequence may be.
Mohammed teaches sounder truth than this—
Tells us that bravery will lead to bliss—
And bravery means character, I trow.
But dear Americus would have us delve
Into his doctrines till the clock strikes twelve.

Avaunt with all such dogmas! they are stale,—
Staler and more antique than yonder vase,
Which bears the marks of centums on its face.
(Americus retaliates.)
You see yon painting hanging near the jet?
A painting of but little merit, yet
I would not part with it for twice its worth;
Because it ever brings to mind the birth
Of hopes and joys and aspirations new,
Such as I never felt till brought to view
By Christ's own face, as witnessed in a dream.
Call it hallucination, if you will,
The sight of that dear face had power to fill
My inmost soul with an ecstatic thrill.
Pedants may worship intellect alone,
Suavely declaring it to be God's throne,
And that all else is but a silhouette.
One's power to think is worthy of respect,
But he who bows to this must needs neglect
The sweeter, broader aspects of the soul,
Where faith and hope and love have full control.
Carlyle was brightest thought personified;
His genius was akin to blades of steel;
But connoisseurs have ever felt to chide
A heart devoid of warmth for human weal.
You call him great withal, and so do I;
But not the greatness that is truly great,
Since faith and hope and love would surely die,
If intellect were judge of man's estate.

(Addressing Menes.)
Reason is monarch of both brain and heart,
Nor would I have you think it otherwise;
But other forces have to act their part,
If man to his full dignity shall rise.
From your remark, dear Menes, one would think
That Christian faith means loss of self respect:
Believe me, sir, it is the missing link
Uniting man to God as His elect.
And am I less a man because of this
Which bids me from my inner life dismiss
All ill, all malice, all unrest and wrong—
So that with heart kept pure I may prolong
A life which otherwise would chafe and fret,
Unless each churlish whim were freely met,
And then—to sink into the grave at last,
With naught to comfort but a selfish past?
No, Menes, no: my faith is not in vain;
I'm all the more a man upon this plane.
(Turning to Thesius.)
I fail to see why you should still distrust
The character of him whose laws are just:
He does not rule through Jupiter nor Mars,
Nor does he condescend to use the stars
As mediums of grace, beyond their light
Which serves to guide the mariner at night.
And as for gods of old Olympic fame—
Esteem them not as gods, except in name,
Else you but bring upon yourself the shame

Which conscience feels so keenly when in blame.
I am surprised, dear Greek, that you should
    think
That death is that from which we all do shrink;
If I but fill my place as does yon flow'r,
I'll look with animation to the hour,
When I shall rise above, beyond that pow'r
Which only offers change and desuetude.
You hate the thought of death, because to you
It has an awful meaning—false or true
You know not which; and the suspense involved
Begets a problem which remains unsolved.
Is not my faith worth more to me than yours
To you, since it beyond all doubt assures
The hope that life beyond the grave shall be
A living verity? Now grant me this!

SECTION V.

7.45 P. M.

In the Greek diplomat's library our three friends are cosily en-
sconsed for further conversation. Thesius is thoughtful beyond his
wont; but Menes preserves the same stolid temperament as on previous
occasions. Americus refers Thesius to the confession of Glaucus to
Sallust in the concluding chapter of Sir Bulwer Lytton's "Last Days of
Pompeii." The scene closes with the absolute refusal of Menes to
accept Christ; but the Greek yields to the gentle persuasiveness of his
friend, and openly avows faith in the Nazarene.

(Thesius receives his friends.)
Well, well, so you have come to do me grace:
And were it possible for me to trace
The time when honored friendships first began,
'Twould surely take us back to primal man,
But after all I find me turning towards
A freer life than Washington affords:
To me the bustle and the constant press
Of social etiquette, I must confess,
Are more distasteful than I dare express.
My books and statuary are to me
Of higher value than society.
Could I but chisel like Praxitiles,
That were a boon of deepest, rarest joy;
But in restraint I cannot be at ease
More than a cornered, hampered, wilful boy.

I love to study life apart from fates,
Whether in tree, or flower, or face of man;
But to be hampered by the mobile traits
Of fashion, is a veritable ban.

           (Turning to Americus.)

I like your city, and your people, too;
Nor would I say one word to injure you,
Whose feelings I respect in very deed.
But after all the truth must now be told;
The new attracts but little, while the old
Supplies the food on which I daily feed.

           (Americus replies.)

Tush, Thesius! your strain does not assuage;
But brings to mind the moods of Chelsea's sage,
Whose pipe was more to him than friendship
    rare.
And as for fossil Greece, I fail to see
The spirit charm of its antiquity.
I know that visions of the past are good;
But do they serve as necessary food
For growth in such a busy age as ours?
Nor have we time to dream of other days,
As on we rush amid the ceaseless maze
Of obligations that do well-nigh craze.

           (Menes speaks.)

I like, for me, the dream life of the East;
Its mellow skies, its tropic fruits, its feast
Of fat things for a sluggish soul like mine:
The trees and flowers ne'er hurry, why should I?

Nor do the flocks e'er worry, but they try
To make the most of each succeeding day.
It rains like fury, or it patters slow;
But no complaint e'er comes from them, you
     know.
And by my faith in Islam, I believe,
That since our mistakes we can ne'er retrieve,
It is better for one to slowly move
Like the tortoise, within a well-worn groove,
Than to rush along at a breakneck speed,
Like a foaming and frenzied battle steed
With no one to curb him, no one to lead!
        (Turning to Americus.)
And such is American life today.
You prate of your prowess, but does it pay,
Is a question that I may justly ask,
Since life is for pleasure and not for task.
    (Americus replies with brow slightly knit.)
To your question I answer yes; and no:
If arrow be shot from a high-strung bow,
'Tis bent to its fullest to give it force,
Lest the arrow fail in its onward course:
After all it is wrong to break the bow
In our ardour to make the arrow go.
         (Thesius speaks.)
You spoke, Americus, of Lytton's book:
What of it, pray? does it contain the meat
A hungry spirit craves? or must I look
For other ground on which to rest my feet?

He speaks of old Pompeii's lifeless form,
Its lore, its beauties, and the fearful storm
That quenched her halcyon light as with a
　　breath,
When plebe and prince were thinking least of
　　death:
But what have these to do with you and me?
'Tis true they teach a moral; but I see
No point that calls for exercise of thought.
　(Thesius pauses a moment then continues.)
Oh, yes—I now perceive the point in view—
The letter Glaucus sent to Sallust, true,
When settled in his own Athenian home,
Refusing as he did to live in Rome,
Despite the welcome of his life long friend.
You mean that part where Glaucus speaks of
　　Christ—
How he with Him had entered into tryst—
Finding sweet fellowship that satisfied
More than Ione's love, though she had tried
To prove her love by standing at his side,
When succor from all sources was denied.
Glaucus was right, I ween, but how shall I
Purchase a friendship which no gold can buy?
Think you, would Christus show his face to me,
As in the dream you had beyond the sea?
I long for something, but I know not what,
To give to life a charm it now has not.
And if *your* Christ will be mine, too, I vow '

To follow Him the rest of life from now.
    (Thesius with face upturned.)
O, blessed thought! Lux Christi, Thou art
    mine!
To Thee my heart, my life, I now resign:
I see Thy face! 'Tis radiant with light,
Such as I never witnessed till this night.
Americus! speak quick! is this the Christ?
And will he condescend with me to tryst,
Forgiving and forgetting all the past,
And over my poor soul His mantle cast?
(Menes rises to depart and evinces perturbance.)
Of all things ill, the illest is no brains
With which to steer what little still remains.
To owe allegiance to the Nazarene,
Is like investing brains at sight, unseen,
Mohammed, prophet of us all! look down
And bless these men with light, that they may
    frown
On such a false belief as Christus taught;
And fill their errant minds with holier thought
Than such as issued from the pseudo-god.
    (Turning to his friends.)
Farewell, my sires, our faith divides us now.
I fain would have it otherwise; but thou,
Americus, dost seek to win me too;
But I shall *not* be won by such as you.
Farewell, dear Greek,—obey your friend's
    behest,

Rely on Christus, if you think it best;
But mark my words,—the gods will give no rest
To such as you.   Adieu, dear Greek, adieu.
(Thesius and Americus alone; Americus speaks.)
Think you, was Menes vexed at what you said?
He acted by the way he tossed his head
As though he thought your talk unwise, absurd.
(Thesius replies.)
I care not what he thought, Americus:
My faith is mine; and when he ranted thus,
I all the more concluded I was right;
And as to following by faith, not sight,
He need not boast, for his is just the same.
'Twas folly then to charge me without cause,
As though his vaunted faith were without flaws,
A faith which at the best is crudely tame.
Instance the Koran with its analects
Of pious cant; and when a man subjects
Himself to such as that,—he should not think
To make me drink at such a fount impure:
I say impure because it fails to give
The draught by which the thirsty soul may live
And thrive and grow until it be mature.
The faith of Islam teaches war—not peace;
Since he who dies in battle will release
All obligations 'twixt himself and God:
Nay, more than this,—the Koran also says
That it alone contains the truth—God's truth,—
And that all else beside is but a lie—

The very soul of infidelity!
Can sword, or smoke of battle make amend
For sins and errors I myself have wrought?
Or, tell me, will the Father condescend
To save me on the strength that I have fought
To guard a fondled creed from perishing?
If Heav'n be won by such a scheme as this,
Then faith means fight, and bloody war means
     bliss.
          (Americus speaks.)
I like to hear you argue thus, old friend,
Because it proves your own sincerity;
And as you now your new found light defend,
'Tis plain you do so with temerity.
Menes were right, if only true to truth;
But being true to error is not right,
Despite the fact that one may be sincere.
Zeus was your God, and you were true to him;
But now that faith, though once so bright, is dim:
Nor would the gods combined, have power to
     move
A faith whose basal principle is love.
Menes must needs devour the ¹*rakhalee*,
Before his troubled soul can be set free
From the delusive spell which holds it now.
He reads the ²Sunna with untiring zeal,
And counts himself more orthodox than we;
He talks with zest of future woe or weal,
And fain would make us think the same as he.

1 **Fruit** peculiar to the jungles of India,—handsome in appearance, but
in taste slimy. 2 Sunna—Moslem traditions.

And now, dear Greek, as I must say good-night,
Be firm in your resolves to make advance:
The way is not obscure, nor is it trite,
To him who searches deeper than a glance.
The way is old, the path well beaten, too,
But what of that so long as it is true.
Truth is worth more than error any day,
Though clothed in garments of the plainest sort;
Its worth is not determined by display,
Nor by the force nor weakness of retort.
Jesus was truth alone personified;
As free from error as the sun is free
To shine without regard to wind or tide;
And this is why He is so much to me.
I too, was far away from God and truth,
Finding no anchor for my restless soul,
Till at the Fountain of perennial youth
I satisfied my thirst, and now am whole.
Had I but slaked my thirst at Error's fount,
Believing only what I could opine,
My theories at best would not amount
To more than delving in an oreless mine.

FINALE.

Oh, Cross divine! divine because of Him,
Whose hands and feet were rudely pierced with
      nails,
By Pariahs who knew not how to love.
Nor could it be that force compelled the deed,
Since this would mean defeat to God himself,
'Twas willingness that made Him bow His head,
To shame and sorrow such as wrung Him through,
That He might prove to us love's truest worth.
A crown of sharpest thorns He meekly bears,
A purple robe and hypocritic ''hail!''
But shall a man be judged by what he wears?
Or do the jibes of ignorance avail?
Only when worth has ceased to be extant,
And truth has abdicated crown and throne,
Only when love is changed to merest cant,
And when the heart has naught to call its own.

Men cut and slash with blades of skeptic steel,
They probe and thrust and lunge at Truth, poor
      fools!
Till, tired of their own folly, they must feel
That they, alas, have been but Satan's tools!
Shine on, Lux Christi, in thy glory mild,
Till darkest nature shall illumined be.
Shine on, dear Light, till all be reconciled
To quit their sins and learn of God through thee.